**Other Yearling Books
by Patricia Reilly Giff You Will Enjoy:**
(Illustrated by Blanche Sims)

YEARLING BOOKS/YOUNG YEARLINGS/YEARLING CLASSICS are designed especially to entertain and enlighten young people. Patricia Reilly Giff, consultant to this series, received the bachelor's degree from Marymount College. She holds the master's degree in history from St. John's University, and a Professional Diploma in Reading from Hofstra University. She was a teacher and reading consultant for many years, and is the author of numerous books for young readers.

For a complete listing of all Yearling titles, write to
Dell Readers Service, P.O. Box 1045,
South Holland, IL 60473.

THE POLKA DOT
PRIVATE EYE

THE TRAIL OF
THE SCREAMING
TEENAGER

Patricia Reilly Giff

Illustrated by Blanche Sims

A YOUNG YEARLING BOOK

Published by
Dell Publishing
a division of
Bantam Doubleday Dell Publishing Group, Inc.
666 Fifth Avenue
New York, New York 10103

ISBN: 0-440-40312-X

Printed in the United States of America

July 1990

10 9 8 7 6 5 4 3 2

CWO

For my Ali,
with love

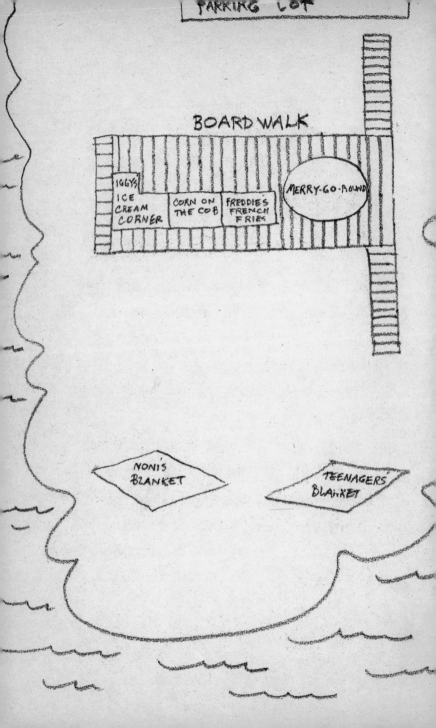

··· CHAPTER ONE ···

Dawn Bosco pulled out an ice cube tray. She banged it against the sink.

Ice cubes flew all over the counter.

She put one in her mouth.

She put another under her Polka Dot Private Eye hat.

"I can't stand it," she told her grandmother, around the ice cube. "It's too hot."

"You're right," said Noni. She fanned herself with her newspaper. She looked out the screen door. "Even Mr. Ott next door is going to the beach."

"Mr. Ott in a bathing suit?" said Dawn. "I can't picture him without his gray suit."

Noni laughed. "Or his fat yellow-striped tie."

Dawn spit out the ice cube. "Hey, that's it. We can go to the beach."

She stood up high on tiptoes. She stretched her arms out in front of her. "Perfect dive by Dawn Tiffanie Bosco."

"Hmmm," said Noni. She rattled her newspaper. Then she nodded. "I'll call Jason's mother. Jill Simon's too. I'll take everyone."

"Yahoo," Dawn yelled. She raced upstairs to her bedroom. She tossed everything out of her dresser.

Her purple-striped bathing suit was in the bottom drawer. It was still a little damp from Emily Arrow's pool the other day.

She fished around for her sunglasses with the mirror eyes.

She poked them on her nose.

They made everything so dark, she could hardly see. "Where am I?" she yelled.

Her cat, Powder Puff, looked up and yawned.

Dawn looked around. What else did she need?

She pulled her Polka Dot Private Eye box out from under her bed.

She blew off the dust.

Maybe she could solve a mystery today.

She stuck her pink bottle of No Sunburn, No Kidding in the box last.

"See you later, Powder Puff," she yelled. "Sorry. No cats allowed at the beach."

She slid down the banister and ran out the door.

Noni was waiting in the car.

She was wearing a big straw hat with an orange flower.

A piece of cardboard was taped to her nose.

Noni hated to get sunburned.

Dawn opened the door. It was a terrible car.

Two fenders were dented. A window was cracked.

It didn't have air conditioning. Not one bit.

"It's as hot as a firecracker!" Dawn said. She slid into the front seat.

"I don't care," said Jason from the back. "All I care about is getting in the water."

Dawn turned around and grinned. "You got here fast."

"In about two minutes," said Jill. She was sitting next to Jason.

Jill had red bows on her four braids.

Two in front, two in back.

Her face was red from the heat.

She looks like a tomato, Dawn thought. A nice red one.

Jill was a great friend.

She was a terrible detective, though.

So was Jason.

"Let's get going," said Noni.

The car rolled down the street.

It rolled slowly.

Dawn's bike could go almost as fast.

"Safe and sound," Noni always said.

"Hurry," Dawn said. "Please." She had to sit with her detective box on her lap.

It was big and square. It was heavy too.

It was filled with great things.

A pair of snap-on handcuffs.

Two fake eyebrows and a furry mustache.

A Polka Dot Private Eye book.

"I'm going to look for a mystery today," Dawn said. She crossed her fingers. "I hope I find one."

Jill leaned forward. "I'm going to look for things in the sand," she said. "Old coins and stuff."

"Hey. Me too," said Dawn. "That's as good as a mystery."

Jill tossed her braids back. "Can I use your—"

Dawn drew in her breath. "Hey." She grabbed Noni's arm. "Hold your horses."

Noni put on the brakes.

Her hat sailed off her head.

"You make me nervous," she told Dawn.

"I forgot something," Dawn said.

"Oh, no," said Jill. "Not the—"

"Yes," said Dawn. "The—"

"I knew it," said Jason. "I'll never get in the water."

Noni backed the car down the street.

They went from one side to the other.

They stopped at Dawn's driveway.

Dawn raced out of the car and into the house.

"Out of my way, please," she shouted to Powder Puff.

She looked under her bed.

She looked behind the curtains . . . and then in the closet.

There it was.

She yanked it out from behind her dollhouse.

It was a long pole with a box on one end.

MARVELOUS METAL FINDER, it said.

It was Noni's old one.

Noni said she was sick of looking for marvelous metal things.

She said she'd rather do her crossword puzzle.

Dawn grabbed the finder. It was perfect for finding pirate coins. Money too.

It was perfect for solving a mystery.

···CHAPTER TWO···

"Look at that water," Dawn said from the boardwalk.

"Look at that sand," said Jason.

"It's a good thing this beach isn't big," said Noni. "I can't walk far in these sandals."

They plodded down the boardwalk steps.

Jason carried a doughnut tube over one arm.

Jill pulled the Marvelous Metal Finder.

Dawn dragged her detective box behind her.

Last came Noni. She tried to keep her straw hat on with one hand.

They looked for a space for their blanket.

The beach was crowded.

Radios were blaring.

People were getting suntans.

"Not too far from the boardwalk," Noni said. "I like to listen to the merry-go-round music."

She spread out their blanket near some teenagers. She plunked down the picnic basket.

One of the teenagers smiled at Dawn.

She had short dark hair and a million freckles.

Dawn smiled back. Then she kicked off her flip-flops. "Last one in the water is a french-fried frog," she yelled.

Jill hopped on the sand. She yanked off one sneaker and tossed it back on the blanket.

She threw off the other one.

"Let me at that water," she yelled.

Jason was blowing up his doughnut tube.

His cheeks looked like purple balloons.

Dawn didn't wait. She ran on tiptoes.

The sand was hot.

Boiling.

"Oooch. Ouch," she yelled.

Noni was yelling too. "You forgot your sunscreen," she said. "Come back."

Dawn stopped on one foot.

"Put it on," said Noni. "You'll be a wrinkled prune by the time you're sixteen."

Dawn ran back to the blanket. She opened her Polka Dot Private Eye box.

She pulled out the fat plastic jar and unscrewed the top.

Then she reached in with four fingers for a big dab of No Sunburn, No Kidding.

At the same time she watched the teen-agers on the next blanket.

There were four of them. Two boys, two girls.

In the middle was the freckled-faced girl.

Next to her was a boy with a radio on his shoulder. He was jerking his head back and forth to the music.

Jason stopped blowing up the doughnut. "He looks like a chicken, doesn't he?"

"Look at the other boy," said Dawn. "The one with hair down to his shoulders."

"Hmpf," said Noni. She liked boys with short hair.

"The blond girl looks cool," said Jason. "Just like a movie star."

Dawn nodded. The girl was wearing a gorgeous silver bathing suit. She had on a sparkly diamond necklace.

She was putting oil on her face, not sunscreen.

Too bad, thought Dawn. She'd be a wrinkled prune any day now.

The blond girl picked up some sand.

She tossed a little on the boy's long hair.

Then she started to run.

"Yeow," she yelled as her feet hit the sand.

Long Hair chased after her.

"Yeow," he yelled too.

He grabbed for the girl as she reached Dawn's blanket.

She twisted away from him.

She landed on top of Dawn.

"Oof," she said.

"Oof," Dawn said too.

Sand sprayed up in the air.

Noni's hat flew off her head.

The No Sunburn jar dropped back into the detective box.

The girl scrambled up. "Sorry," she yelled.

She hopped across the sand toward a little boy. A kindergarten boy, Dawn thought.

About forty-nine toys were piled up on his blanket.

His mother was scrunched up in the middle. She was reading a book.

The boy was building a sand hill.

It was almost as big as he was.

The girl's foot smashed into it.

The boy began to roar. He picked up his shovel and threw it at her.

The girl leapt away from him.

On the next blanket a man was sitting behind his newspaper.

The girl bumped into his beach chair.

She waved at him, then bounced up the steps to the boardwalk.

"Well!" Noni told Dawn. "I hope you have better manners."

Dawn hopped up. "I do, I do."

She slammed down the cover of her detective box. She raced across the sand and dived into the water.

It was cool, salty, wonderful.

Behind her came the kindergarten kid and his mother.

She was still reading. She was holding the book up in the air.

The book was getting wet anyway.

The boy looked at Dawn. He pulled back his arm. Then he splashed her as hard as he could.

"Arno," said the mother without looking at him, "I don't think that was very friendly."

Dawn scrunched up her nose. She'd like to give Arno a quick punch.

Dawn looked around for Jill and Jason.

16

One of Jill's bows was floating on the water.

Jill was floating too.

Jason was swimming in the doughnut tube. "Great," he yelled.

Dawn lay on her back. She kicked her feet. "I love to float," she said. "I learned it at camp."

She closed her eyes. If only she had a mystery to solve.

Then she thought she heard something. "Is someone yelling?" she began, and got a mouthful of water.

"Everyone's yelling," Jill said.

Dawn kicked once more. Then she stood up to see what was happening.

On the boardwalk, the merry-go-round was going around.

In front was the sand and umbrellas and people sitting on blankets.

She could see Noni bent over her crossword puzzle . . . and the teenagers standing near her.

The girl with the long blond hair was standing on her blanket.

And she was screaming as loud as she could.

···CHAPTER THREE···

Dawn rode in on a wave.

She scrambled up on the sand.

The girl was still screaming.

She waved her arms around.

Even Noni looked up from her crossword puzzle to watch.

Dawn shook the water out of her hair. She raced for the blanket.

"Wait for me," yelled Jill.

Dawn didn't stop. She had to see what was going on.

Besides, poor Jill wouldn't be any help at all.

"It's gone," the girl said. She was wringing her hands. "My almost-diamond necklace with the two almost-ruby hearts."

The chicken-head boy with the radio clicked his teeth.

"It must have fallen off," said the freckle-faced girl.

"We'll look all over the place," Long Hair said. "We'll dig in the sand around the blanket."

The blond girl shook her head. "I bet someone picked it up. That makes someone a thief." She opened her mouth. "Help. Someone's a thief."

The other teenagers shook their heads. They searched through the blanket.

They scooped up the sand around them.

Dawn crept closer.

"Help," the girl yelled again.

"I'll help," said Dawn.

The girl stopped screaming. "You're just a little kid."

Dawn drew herself up. "I'm the Polka Dot Private Eye. I've solved at least eight cases."

"Seven," said Jill from behind her.

"Six," said Jason.

"Anyway," said Dawn, "I'm ready to solve this one too."

She reached for her Polka Dot Private Eye hat. "Tell me the clues."

"No clues. Not one," said the girl. "I had it on the blanket. I didn't have it on the boardwalk." She opened her mouth wide. "Thieeeeef."

"What's your name?" Dawn asked.

"Mindy Merrill," said the girl. "I made it up myself. I want to be an actress."

Dawn frowned. "But what's your real name?"

The girl frowned too. She opened her mouth. "Glad—"

Just then someone else started to scream. Someone up on the boardwalk.

"Gladys Gump," yelled a boy with brown hair and glasses, "if you don't get home right this minute, Mom's going to kill you."

"My brother," said the girl. "I have to go home."

She looked around one last time. "It's a great necklace," she said. "The rubies shine in the dark."

"Did you hear me?" the boy shouted. "Time to go home."

The girl shook out her shoes.

She put on a blue flowered hat.

"There's a reward," she said.

"How much?" asked Dawn and Jason together.

The girl raised one shoulder. "A quarter, I guess."

"I think I'm going to look for pirate coins instead," said Jill.

"Now," yelled the boy. "I'm going without you."

"My brother has no patience." She looked at Dawn. "Try to find the thief."

Dawn nodded. "I'll look for coins later." She shook her head. "How about your address?"

"One twelve–thirty-two . . . Never mind. I'll be back tomorrow." The girl hopped over Noni's red plaid blanket.

She stepped in front of the man's newspaper.

She made a wide circle around the kindergarten kid.

He threw another shovel at her anyway.

Then she disappeared up on the boardwalk.

"Terrific," said Dawn. "We've got a mystery."

"Not so terrific," said Noni. "She got sand all over my crossword puzzle."

Dawn put on her sunglasses with the mirror eyes. She didn't want anyone to see her watching.

Then she looked around.

The man was still reading his newspaper.

Long Hair and Freckle Face were digging around in the sand.

Chicken Head was clucking in time to his radio.

"Someone here is probably a thief," Dawn

said. "And we're going to catch him. Or her."

Jill Simon shivered. She clapped her hands over her look-like-real pearl necklace.

"I think I know what we should do next," she said.

Dawn looked up.

"Eat lunch," said Jill. "I'm starved."

···CHAPTER FOUR···

Dawn ate her egg-salad sandwich on rye bread. "Nice and crunchy," she said.

"That's sand." Noni smiled. "It's all over you."

"I don't mind." Dawn reached for a peach. Then she sat back and tried to think.

How could she solve the mystery of the almost-diamond necklace?

She could see Jason was thinking too.

"I bet it's the man with the newspaper," he said. "He kept hiding behind it."

"He probably didn't want to get sunburned," said Noni. "Or maybe he wanted some peace and quiet too."

"Maybe," said Jason. "I'm going to keep an eye on him anyway."

Jill nodded. Her mouth was filled with a chocolate-chip cookie.

She had two more cookies in each hand.

"I gluf fo fem," she said.

"I think she's saying she loves to eat," said Jason.

Jill shook her head.

"What are you saying?" Dawn asked.

"Wait till she finishes," said Noni. "Better manners that way."

Dawn looked up at the sky. "Who could have stolen it?"

"I don't nof," said Jill.

"Me neither." Dawn sat up straight. "Wait a minute. I do know."

"Whooof?"

"I *almost* know." Dawn nodded to herself. "Now, listen. Mindy was wearing the necklace on the blanket. It was gone when she got to the boardwalk. Right?"

"Right," said Jason.

Dawn narrowed her eyes. "It had to be someone in between."

She raised her fingers in the air. "Suspects," she said. "First: the man with the newspaper."

"Told you," said Jason.

Dawn nodded. "Or maybe one of the other teenagers."

Jill swallowed. "I'm trying to say that maybe—"

"That chicken-head kid looks like a thief if I ever saw one," Dawn said.

"What about that little kid?" Jason asked.

"Yes," Dawn said. "That bratty kindergarten kid, Arno."

Jill stood up. "I'm glad you didn't say us."

Dawn sighed. "Of course I didn't."

"Just joking." Jill reached for the Marvelous Metal Finder. "Anyway, I was going to say that the necklace may just be lost."

"Not stolen?" Dawn said. "Don't be silly."

Jill raised one shoulder. "I'm going to look anyway. I'm going to look for coins too."

She swept across the sand with the finder. *Buzz, click.*

"It works." Jill sifted through the sand and pulled out a penny.

"Great," said Noni. "It's a 1962 penny. That was a year that John Kennedy was president."

Dawn looked at the Marvelous Metal Finder. "Keep looking. Maybe you'll find the necklace." She leaned over the blanket.

"There's something I have to do right away."

Jason leaned forward. "What?"

"I'm going to lock my Polka Dot Private Eye box. No thief is going to get my good stuff."

She tapped Noni's knee.

Noni reached into her pocket. She pulled out a pink heart lock and a silver key.

Dawn snapped the lock on the private eye box. She piled the lunch box on top of it . . . and her flip-flops . . . and her wet pink towel.

Buzz, click.

"Hey," said Jill. "A nail."

"Hey," said Jason at the same time. "There goes the man with the newspaper."

Dawn didn't stop to look. "Follow that man," she yelled.

They scrambled up and started to run.

Dawn glanced down at the man's blanket.

Nothing was on it, though.

Nothing but the newspaper.

She reached out with one toe and flipped the paper over.

A banana was underneath.

So was a pack of Chiclets.

No almost-diamond necklace with two almost-ruby hearts.

"Hurry," yelled Jason. "I can hardly see him anymore."

Dawn stood on tiptoes. "I can't see him at all."

They circled around the kindergarten kid.

Dawn hopped over his red-and-blue sand pail.

"You're going to get it," he said. "Any minute."

Up on the boardwalk there was music.

The merry-go-round was going around.

"There he is," whispered Jason.

Dawn looked. The man was sitting on the tallest horse.

He had on a yellow-striped bathing suit.

A yellow sweatband was pulled down over his forehead.

"That's the man?" Dawn asked, shaking her head. "Are you sure?"

Jason nodded. "I'm positive."

The man waved at them. "Love the merry-go-round," he called. "Always did."

"Good grief," said Dawn. "That's no thief."

"How do you know?" asked Jason.

"It's Mr. Ott from next door."

···CHAPTER FIVE···

"I didn't think he was the thief," said Dawn.

Jason looked disappointed. "There goes my suspect."

"Isn't it time for ice cream?" said a voice behind them.

It was Jill. Only two red bows were left on her braids.

She was carrying a green jar.

She rattled it. "I found a nickel," she

said. "It has a picture of Jefferson's head, and his house on the back. Some house."

Dawn looked toward the beach. She was dying to find some stuff.

"I found a key," Jill went on, "and a couple of nails."

"Lucky," said Dawn.

"No necklace, though."

Jill held out some money. "From Noni for ice cream."

Dawn thought for a second. "I guess we have time for a quick— "

"Very quick—" Jason added.

Jill smiled. "—ice cream cone."

They marched along the boardwalk . . . past the hot-corn-on-the-cob stand . . . past Freddie's French Fries.

They turned in at Iggy's Ice Cream Corner.

Dawn took a deep breath. "Look. There's Chicken Head and Long Hair."

"Freckle Face too," said Jason.

"They're having my favorite ice cream," said Jill. "Chocolate double-dip Oreo crunch."

Dawn stopped. She handed Jason her money. "Get me an orange raspberry," she said. "There's something I have to do. Right away."

She raced back along the boardwalk, down onto the beach.

Stepping along, she raised her feet high in the air.

The sand was as hot as Freddie's french fries.

She looked at her blanket.

Noni wasn't there.

She could see Noni's big straw hat bobbing along down near the water.

Dawn looked around. Then she tiptoed to the teenagers' blanket.

Stuff was piled up all over the place.

Sand was too.

Dawn glanced toward the boardwalk.

She had to work fast.

She had to search the blanket before the teenagers came back.

She started at one corner.

She shook out one size-twelve sneaker. She shook out another one.

Nothing was in them.

Next she shook out the towels. They were wet and sandy.

She hated to touch them.

She tilted the picnic basket to see underneath.

No almost-diamond necklace . . . but plenty of sand.

These teenagers certainly were messy.

Only one place was left. Inside the picnic basket . . . in with the lunch.

She opened the lid. It was crammed

with half-eaten sandwiches and two apple cores.

Yucks.

She picked up a sandwich to look underneath.

Just then she heard shouting. The voices were angry.

"What's that kid doing? Stop, thief!"

She looked up.

Maybe someone had solved the crime ahead of her.

Long Hair and Chicken Head were coming down the boardwalk steps.

They were pointing . . . pointing at her . . . racing toward her.

She dropped the sandwich back into the basket.

She slammed the lid.

Then she scrambled up. "Noni, save me," she yelled.

She looked around.

Noni was way down at the end of the beach.

Jason and Jill were nowhere in sight.

"When I get my hands on you . . ." Long Hair yelled.

Dawn started to run.

She darted around a green beach blanket, circled a litter basket, and headed for the water.

She could hardly catch her breath.

She looked back over her shoulder.

Chicken Head had stopped at the blanket. He was checking out the picnic basket.

Long Hair was still after her.

And he was closer. Much closer.

Dawn put on a burst of speed. She ran along the water's edge.

Waves lapped against her feet.

"Noni," she yelled again.

41

Noni's hat bobbed along. She was still a long way away.

"Someone help me," Dawn yelled.

No one even paid attention.

She looked back once more . . . and fell.

Her nose and cheeks scratched against the sand.

A big hand grabbed her shoulder.

···CHAPTER SIX···

Dawn scrambled up. She had sand in her eyes and in her mouth.

It tasted gritty against her teeth.

She tried to talk. "I didn't take anything," she said at last.

She kept her eyes closed and rubbed at them with two fingers.

"You're a thief," said a voice.

She opened one eye. She could see long brown hair.

She could see something else too.

Chicken Head had come down toward the

water. He was hopping up and down, listening to the radio on his shoulder.

He was jerking his head back and forth.

He was making *cluck, cluck* noises with his teeth.

Dawn drew herself up as tall as she could. She watched for Noni with one eye. "I am the Polka Dot Private Eye," she said.

Chicken Head stopped clucking. "Then I am Princess Di," he said.

He began to laugh at his joke, slapping his knee.

The girl with the freckles was coming toward them. "Did you hurt yourself?" she asked.

Dawn felt like crying.

She didn't, though.

Detectives never cry.

She shook her head. "No."

Sand flew all over the place.

"We caught the thief," said Long Hair.

"Cluckity-cluck," said Chicken Head.

"Ridiculous," said the girl. She wiped sand off Dawn's forehead. "You didn't take the necklace, did you?"

"Of course not," said Dawn. "I solve crimes."

She wanted to ask if the girl had taken the necklace.

She'd probably hurt her feelings, though.

Too bad. She had to do it.

Right was right. That's what Noni always said.

She opened her mouth.

She could see Jason and Jill coming toward her.

Jason was carrying a drippy ice cream cone in each hand.

Jill had chocolate ice cream all over her mouth.

46

They were running as fast as they could.

They were weaving around blankets and litter baskets.

The kindergarten kid threw a pail at them.

His mother didn't even look up.

"We're coming to save you," Jason yelled. "Don't worry."

"Hold on," yelled Jill. Her last bow sailed off her head.

Dawn looked at the teenage girl. "Did you take—"

At the same time the girl shook her finger at the other teenagers. "This little girl never took our almost-diamond necklace. Look how sweet she is."

"Our almost-diamond necklace?" Dawn said slowly.

The girl waved her hand. "We gave it to Gladys . . . I mean Mindy . . . for her birthday."

"Cluckity-cluck," said Chicken Head, bobbing with the music.

Long Hair pushed his hair out of his eyes. "Had to work three hours at the dry cleaner's for my share."

Just then Jason plowed into them. "Watch out," he yelled to Chicken Head. "The police are coming."

The ice cream flew out of the cones.

They landed on Long Hair's feet.

"These kids are wacko," Long Hair yelled. He raced for the water.

"Cluckity-cluckity-cluck," said Chicken Head. He danced back to the blanket.

The girl reached into a pocket. "Here's a dollar," she said. "Get yourself another ice cream."

"No, thanks." Dawn smiled at the girl. "I have a mystery to solve."

Jill picked up the Marvelous Metal Finder.

"Here I go again. I'm still looking for that necklace, don't worry."

She began to sweep.

Buzz, *click*.

"Another penny," Jill yelled. "Nineteen fifty-two. That's old!"

Dawn shook her head. "This whole mystery is taking longer than I thought."

She looked toward the kindergarten kid.

They had saved the worst suspect for last.

···CHAPTER SEVEN···

Noni came puffing up to them. "Wonderful walk," she said. She looked at her watch. "I think it's time to go home."

Dawn shook her head. "We can't. We have to check out one more—"

"Your mother will be home from work soon." Noni bent down. She reached for the picnic basket. "Your father too."

Dawn looked back at the kindergarten kid.

He was burying his mother in the sand.

Her face was sticking out of the sand. Her arm holding her book was too. So was one toe.

"If we don't check on this now," said Dawn, "it'll be too late."

"I have to peel potatoes," Noni said. "I have to slice cucumbers."

"Five minutes," said Dawn. "Just five quick minutes."

"Five minutes," Jill begged too. "I haven't found one pirate coin. I haven't found the necklace either."

Buzz, click went the detector.

"A pink bottle-cap," she said.

Noni sat down. She smiled at them. "All right. A fast five minutes."

Dawn nodded. She was still watching Arno, the kindergarten boy.

He was covering his mother's toe.

Dawn and Jason marched toward him.

He looked back over his shoulder.

He picked up a shovel.

Dawn raced back to Jill. "Can I borrow a nickel?"

Jill reached into her green jar. She pulled out a greenish-looking nickel.

Dawn tossed it up in the air.

She wanted to be sure the kindergarten kid could see it.

She walked over and held it out toward him.

At the same time she tried to check out his blanket.

It was hard to see with his toys all over the place.

"Turn the page for me, someone," said the mother. "Please."

Dawn reached over and turned the page.

Arno was smashing the sand down around his mother's toes.

"Listen, Arno . . ." Dawn began.

"Nice burying job," said Jason at the same time.

The boy stopped pounding with his shovel. He looked at the nickel. "That's from the jar?" he asked.

"It's for you," Dawn said. She handed it to him. "I want to ask you about a necklace."

The boy waved the nickel in the air. "What else is in the bottle?"

Dawn rolled her eyes.

She went back to Jill. "Could I borrow the jar, please?"

Jill laughed. "Why not? This beach is full of stuff."

Dawn walked back to Arno. She rattled the jar.

He held out his hand, looked inside, and dumped out half of it on the blanket.

Dawn leaned over. She tried to make him pay attention. "I'm looking for a necklace."

Arno mounded more sand up on his mother's feet.

"I'm going to make an apartment house," he said. "Right here on top of my mother."

"It's an almost-diamond necklace," Dawn said.

"It has two ruby hearts," said Jason.

The boy sat back. "I think I'll dump some water here. I'll make it a little squishy."

He kicked at his pail. He pointed to Jason. "You can get it," he said.

"No, thanks," said Jason.

"No answer," said the boy.

Jason started for the water. "Some kid," he said over his shoulder.

His mother waved her book around. "You're telling me."

Dawn leaned closer. "Come on, kid. What's your name?"

"Killer," he said.

His mother started to laugh. "Come on, Arno. Be serious."

"Listen, Arno," said Dawn. "What about the necklace?"

"No." He shook his head. "You think I play with girls' stuff?"

His mother opened her other eye. "One thing I have to say about Arno. He tells the truth. Another thing. He doesn't like girls' stuff."

Arno piled sand on his shovel. "What a dummy," he said. "You'd better get out of here."

"Turn the page first," said the mother. "Thanks."

Dawn bent over. She flipped the page.

Arno tossed the shovelful of sand at her knees.

Dawn took a deep breath.

She wished she were Arno's mother for two minutes.

She went back to the blanket.

Noni was gathering everything together.

Jill was making one last sweep with the Marvelous Metal Finder. "Bad news," she said. "The necklace isn't here. Definitely."

···CHAPTER EIGHT···

Dawn still had sand in her hair, sand in her ears, sand all over.

She blasted water into the tub. She waited until it was almost to the top.

Then she dumped in half a bottle of Beautiful Bubbles for Beauties.

She made sure the door was locked.

Noni would have a fit if she saw the bubbles sloshing out of the tub.

She didn't bother to take off her bathing suit.

That was filled with sand too.

She hopped in and started to sing.

Then she stopped.

What was the matter with her?

She had to solve a mystery.

She had to solve it fast . . . before tomorrow when they saw Mindy Merrill again.

She put her head back. Her hair floated out around her.

She sighed. No one was left to be the thief.

No one was the thief.

She closed one eye.

Maybe the necklace had fallen in the sand.

She thought about it.

No. Definitely not.

Jill would have found it with the Marvelous Metal Finder.

This whole thing was a puzzle.

She shook her head.

Water splashed into her ear. "Glug," she said.

She jumped up.

She climbed out of the tub and hopped on one foot.

Noni shouted up from downstairs. "What's going on?"

"An ocean is in my ear," Dawn yelled.

"What?"

The water trickled out.

"Don't worry," Dawn yelled. "It's on the floor now."

She looked in the mirror.

Her hair was all snarled.

Jill wasn't the thief.

Jason wasn't the thief.

Only one person was left.

Dawn Tiffanie Bosco.

How terrible.

How ridiculous.

She sat on the edge of the tub.

She stirred the water with one foot.

She had to think out loud.

"Girl wearing a necklace. Girl running. Boy chasing. Necklace gone. Not in the sand. Not in newspaper. Not teenager. Not Arno. . . . Wait a minute."

There was something. Something with Jill. Something with her polka dot box. Something with pink.

What was it?

Someone banged on the bathroom door.

It was her brother Chris.

He was home from baseball camp.

"Are you talking to yourself?" he called.

"I'm solving a mystery," she said.

She stirred the water one more time.

"YEOW." She pulled the plug. "I've got it."

She grabbed a towel and dried her feet.

She wrung out her bathing suit and dressed as fast as she could.

She charged downstairs.

Noni was washing watercress.

"That stuff makes me shiver," Dawn said.

Noni popped a leaf into her mouth. "Uhm, wonderful," she said.

"Where's my Polka Dot Private Eye box?" Dawn asked. "I need it right away. This minute."

Noni pointed with her foot. "On the back step," she said. "It's all sandy."

Dawn opened the back door. She began to drag in the box.

"Don't . . ." Noni began, and sighed. Too late.

A trail of sand followed Dawn across the kitchen floor.

Dawn stopped at the kitchen table.

"I need to get something," she said. "Something to solve the mystery."

She sat back on her heels.

"Uh-oh. The box is locked."

Noni put another piece of watercress in her mouth. "Of course it is. I gave you the lock."

Dawn raised her hands. "But where's the key?"

···CHAPTER NINE···

Dawn yanked on her purple-striped bathing suit. It was her favorite.

It was still wet from yesterday.

So what!

Maybe she could solve the mystery today. She pulled a comb through her hair.

She'd solve it if Arno was at the beach.

And then she'd have time to find some coins . . . special ones.

She grabbed her detective box and headed for the car.

Arno, that killer kid, had the key.

She was sure of it.

Last night she and Jill had gone through Jill's green jar.

Jill had a million things. Pennies, nails, an old silver pen, a sandy pink bottle-cap, and a watch that didn't work.

"I know I had a key in there," Jill had said, frowning. "No old coins, but a silver key. A little silver—"

"My little—" Dawn had said.

Right now Dawn marched across the beach ahead of Noni.

She was dragging her Polka Dot Private Eye box.

Jason and Jill were way ahead of them.

"Here," said Noni.

Dawn backed up.

She threw off her flip-flops.

The teenagers were there.

Any minute Gladys-Mindy would ask about the necklace.

Arno was there too.

He was standing on top of a pile of sand. "I am the king," he shouted.

Dawn marched up to him. "You are the king with my key. I need it back. Please."

"Tough," he said. He patted his pocket.

Dawn stood up straight. "I am the Polka Dot Private Eye. I have a mystery to solve."

Arno's eyes opened wide. "Why didn't you say so?"

He reached into his pocket and pulled out a sandy key.

Dawn raced back to her blanket.

Arno raced behind her.

Jill and Jason were waiting.

Even Noni looked up from her crossword puzzle.

"Now, ladies and gentlemen," said Dawn. "You will see . . ."

Mindy hopped across the sand toward them. "My necklace?" she called.

"You will see . . ." Dawn began again. She pulled the detective box closer.

She turned the key in the lock.

Arno stuck his nose over her shoulder as she flipped open the lid.

She opened her mouth. "Yucks, what a mess."

"Ick-o," said Arno.

"What happened?" asked Jill.

Dawn looked. The inside was covered with pink glop.

"I was afraid of this," she said.

She reached out. "May I have your green jar?" she asked Jill.

Jill handed it over.

Dawn fished through it.

She held up a sandy pink bottle-cap.

"This belongs to my No Sunburn, No Kidding jar," she said.

"That's the whole mystery?" Arno asked.

Dawn sighed. "Give me time."

She stuck her hand in the pink glop.

She pulled out a furry pink mustache.

She yanked out a furry pink eyebrow.

And then . . . she pulled out an almost-diamond necklace . . . covered with pink glop.

"My necklace," yelled Mindy. "Terrific."

"But how . . ." Jill said.

"I was putting on my No Sunburn, No Kidding," said Dawn.

"Good girl," said Noni.

"Mindy hopped over the blanket," Dawn went on. "She hopped over me."

"The necklace fell off . . ." Jill said.

"And landed in the box," said Dawn.

Arno tapped Mindy on the shoulder. "The important thing, no kidding, is the reward."

Mindy smiled. She reached into her purse. She handed Dawn a coin.

"A quarter."

"Let's buy me ice cream," said Arno.

Mindy shook her head. "Look at it closely."

Dawn held it up. "Nineteen seventy-six."

"It's special," said Mindy, "for the two-hundredth anniversary of this country."

"Liberty quarter," said Dawn.

"Lucky," said Jill.

Arno picked up the Marvelous Metal Finder. "Let's find some more."

"Wait a minute," said a voice behind them.

Dawn looked up. She could see a man holding a newspaper. A man with knobby knees.

"How about a merry-go-round ride?" said the man.

"Why not?" said Dawn. She smiled at Mr. Ott. "Let's do it before something else happens around here."